P9-CFU-405

THE TALE OF THE LUCKY CAT

幸運貓的故事

Retold and illustrated by
SUNNY SEKI

故事重述及插圖：SUNNY SEKI

Chinese translation by Zeng Fan　曾凡　翻譯

East West Discovery Press

Manhattan Beach, California

This book is dedicated to my parents, brother, wife, nine children, and our cat.
- S.S

Text and illustrations copyright © 2007 by East West Discovery Press
Chinese translation copyright © 2008 by East West Discovery Press

Published by:
East West Discovery Press
P.O. Box 3585, Manhattan Beach, CA 90266
Phone: 310-545-3730, Fax: 310-545-3731
Website: www.eastwestdiscovery.com

Written and illustrated by Sunny Seki
Chinese translation by Zeng Fan
Chinese proofreading by Icy Smith
Edited by Marcie Rouman
Book production by Luzelena Rodriguez
Production management by Icy Smith

ISBN-13: 978-0-9669437-8-8 Hardcover
Library of Congress Control Number: 2007937876
First Bilingual English and Chinese Edition 2008
Printed in China
Published in the United States of America

The Tale of the Lucky Cat is also available in English only and eight bilingual editions including English with Arabic, Chinese, Hmong, Japanese, Korean, Spanish, Tagalog and Vietnamese.

Japanese Glossary/日本詞彙:
Tama: A round object/圓的物體
Sensei: A respectful word for teacher/對老師的尊稱
Osho: Leader of a Buddhist temple/佛廟里的長老
Osho-san: The respectful and friendly way to address the *osho*/
對佛廟里的長老尊敬友好的稱謂
Kokoro: The mind or spirit of a living thing/生物的精靈
Maneki: Inviting or beckoning/邀請或點頭招呼
Neko: Cat/貓

A long time ago in Japan, there lived a toymaker named Tokuzo. He was a kind young man who traveled from village to village to sell his toys at festivals.

很久以前，在日本有個做玩具的善良的青年人，名字叫德旦。在節日時候，他從這個村莊走到另一個村莊，出售自己製作的玩具。

3

Children liked his toys. Still, Tokuzo was making barely enough money to survive. "Someday," he thought, "I'll create something so unique that everyone will want to have it."

孩子們都喜歡他的玩具。可是德旦還是難以維持生活。他想，「終有一天，我會創造出一個非常特殊的人人都想要得到的東西。」

The next festival was big, and Tokuzo knew that he would be able to sell a lot of toys there. So he was in a hurry to get the best place. He started on his journey, but had no idea that soon his life was about to change.

　　一個盛大的節日馬上要來臨，德旦知道他能夠賣出很多的玩具，但是他必須趕到最好的地方去。他立刻上路，一點也不知道他的生活將很快發生變化。

He had just entered a small village, when suddenly a frightened cat darted past him. It was being chased by a growling dog.

"Oh, no! Stop!" Tokuzo screamed because he saw an express-delivery horse speeding in their direction. He stood helplessly as the horse hit the cat.

他剛剛走進一個小村莊，忽然看見一隻驚恐的貓從他身邊跑過，一條咆哮的凶狗在後面緊緊追趕。

「站住！停下！」德旦大聲的喊，因為他看見一匹送快遞的郵馬正朝著貓跑的方向奔過去。德旦毫無辦法站在那兒，眼看著大馬踢中了小貓。

The accident happened so quickly that the townspeople did not notice the cat at all. But Tokuzo saw that it had been badly hurt.

"Maybe I can save it. It's still breathing," he said. He quickly found an inn, and carried the cat inside.

事件發生在一瞬間，村裡的人們根本沒有注意到小貓，只有德旦知道小貓受了重傷。

「小貓還有一口氣，也許我可以救活它。」德旦這樣說道，迅速找到一家小旅店，把小貓抱進去。

That night, Tokuzo stayed up late. He wrapped the cat's broken leg and made sure that the bed was warm and clean. "I'll name you 'Tama' – just like the round bell you are wearing," said Tokuzo.

那天晚上，德旦久久沒有睡覺。他把貓的傷腿包扎好，給小貓弄了個乾淨暖和的床。德旦說：「我就叫你圓圓，因為你就像那個掛在你身上的圓鈴鐺。」

The next morning, Tama opened its eyes and seemed to smile.

"Good, Tama. I am so relieved. Today is the big festival, but I'm going to stay behind in this small town with you instead. I want to be sure that you get well."

第二天早上，圓圓睜開眼睛，似乎在微笑。

「你好些了，圓圓，我真是松了一口氣。今天是個重大的節日，但是我決定留在這個小鎮裡和你在一起，我要照顧你等你康復。」

The following day, Tokuzo was able to sell a few toys to the village children. With the little money he earned, he bought two fish: one for himself, and one for Tama. "Tonight we'll celebrate!" he thought.

He returned to the inn and opened the door. "Tama…" he called. However, when he lit the candle, he discovered that Tama had died.

那天德旦僅僅賣給村裡孩子們幾件玩具，他用所得的錢買了兩條魚，一條自己吃，一條給圓圓。他想：「今晚我們要慶祝節日。」

他回到旅店開了門。「圓圓…」，他叫道，點亮油燈，卻發現圓圓已經死去。

The next morning, Tokuzo buried Tama in a grave overlooking the broad countryside. His heart was heavy with grief as he said goodbye.

第二天早晨，德旦把圓圓埋在一個高地上，從那裡可以俯視廣闊的田野。德旦非常悲傷，心情沉重地和圓圓告別。

The big festival was almost over, but Tokuzo still had time. So he continued on his journey. Suddenly the sky grew dark. Rumbling thunder warned that a rainstorm was coming fast.

盛大的節日就要結束，德旦還可以趕上個尾聲，他繼續趕路。忽然天空變黑，隆隆的雷聲預示著暴風雨即將來臨。

He quickly ran to the closest tree for cover. The rain started to pour harder and harder.

德旦急忙跑到一棵大樹下避雨，這時雨點越來越大越來越急。

As Tokuzo wiped his face, he noticed a cat meowing by the temple gate. It seemed to be inviting him to come inside! Surprisingly, this cat looked like Tama, who had died just the day before.

就在德旦擦去臉上雨水的時候，忽然看見一只小貓在一座廟門口喵喵的叫，好像在招呼德旦過去。令德旦吃驚的是那只貓非常像昨天死去的圓圓。

Tokuzo forgot about the rain. He ran toward the cat. "Tama, Tama… is that you? What are you doing here? I thought you died!" He had almost touched the cat, when suddenly…

德旦忘記了大雨，向小貓跑去，「圓圓，圓圓… 是你嗎？ 你在這兒幹甚麼？ 我以為你死了。」就在德旦剛剛要摸到圓圓的那一瞬間，突然…

BAM! There was a huge explosion of light and sound. He turned around and gasped. The pine tree that had protected him from the rain had been split in half by a powerful bolt of lightning!

「砰 」爆發出一聲巨響，一道閃光，德旦轉身看，氣都透不出來，那棵給德旦遮雨的大松樹被雷電擊中劈成兩半。

Tokuzo told everyone how a mysterious cat had saved him. The people were amazed at this story. They could not believe it. "How can cats know that lightning is going to strike? And if cats are dead, how can they call you?"

Tokuzo did not know how to answer. "I am sure that cat saved my life, but I have no way to prove it to you."

The *Osho-San* was listening carefully at the temple. "Maybe there is some truth here that we cannot explain. Tokuzo, please spend the night with us at the temple so that we can talk about it."

德旦逢人就講神秘的貓是怎樣救了他命的故事。人們非常驚奇，他們不能夠相信，貓怎麼會知道雷電會劈下來，況且已經死了的貓怎麼會召喚呢？

德旦也不知道該怎樣回答。「我確信是那只貓救了我的命，但是我不知道如何向你們來證明它。」

廟裡的老和尚仔細聽了這個故事。「也許真有那麼回事兒，但是我們不能夠解釋。德旦，請到廟裡來過夜，我們可以好好談談。」

He went to the meditation garden to think. "I was saved by Tama, and the people didn't believe it. What am I supposed to do next? I should create a statue of this cat," he thought, "so everybody can share my good luck."

He asked the *Osho-san* for advice. "Let me introduce you to Old Master Craftsman. His daughter takes care of him because he is not well. But he is wise, and will tell you what you should do."

德旦到了靜思園獨自想，「圓圓救了我的命，但是人們不相信，我應該怎麼辦呢？我要給圓圓建一個雕塑，這樣人人都能夠分享我的運氣。」

德旦向老和尚請教，老和尚說：「我把你介紹給老工匠，他是個非常聰明的人，會告訴你應該怎麼做。不過老工匠現在身體不好，他的女兒在照顧他。」

One fine morning, Old Master was feeling a little better, and he came out to watch. He was impressed by Tokuzo's determination. "Your cats are looking much better. Now, why don't you make the arm swing by hiding a weight inside the body?" he ked. "The cleverest ideas are often hidden behind what the eye can see."

Tokuzo jumped up, amazed. "Yes! That will make the cat seem more alive. Thank so much, *Sensei*!" Now Old Master started to get excited, too.

個晴朗的早晨，老工匠身體好些了，他來到作坊看，被德旦的決心感動，
「你的貓看上去好多了，為甚麼你不讓貓舉起一只爪，它的重心就藏到身
你知道嗎？最聰明的想法往往就隱藏在最吸引目光的地方。」
興的跳起來，「真了不起！這樣看起來我的貓就更活靈活現了！老師傅，
指教。」現在老工匠也為這個雕塑感到興奮。

He brought his work to Old Master Craftsman. "This can be a nice-looking cat, young man. But you did not mix the clay well, and the fire was too hot," he said.

Tokuzo would not give up. He needed more firewood, so he went back to the tree that had been struck by lightning. He started over again, and worked day and night.

德旦把碎塊帶給老工匠看。老工匠說：「這本可以是個很好看的貓，可惜你的泥和不夠好，另外你的爐火太熱了。」

德旦可不會半途而廢。他需要更多的木柴，就到那棵被雷電劈倒的大樹去收集。他從頭做起，夜以繼日地加緊工作。

Finally, the clay was baked! Tokuzo reached for the oven door, and peered down at his work. He couldn't believe his eyes. "Look at my cats! What did I do wrong?" His carefully formed statues had cracked and shattered into pieces.

終於，泥胎烘烤好了。德旦順著爐門望裡窺看，簡直不敢相信自己的眼睛。「看看我的貓，甚麼地方出了錯?」他仔仔細細製作的泥胎破裂開，成了一堆碎塊。

He started to follow Old Master's directions. First, he had to mix the clay.

按照老工匠的指點，首先要和泥。

Then, he had to form it into the shape of a cat. "These don't look like cats at all!" he told himself.

然後他把泥塑成貓的形狀。「這可一點都不像貓!」德旦自言自語。

Next, the clay had to be baked so that it could harden. But to start a fire, first wood had to be cut. This was much more work than he had expected.

下一步，要烘烤泥胎，讓它變硬。要烘烤，首先要點火，要點火，就要準備木柴，工作很多，比他原先想的要多。

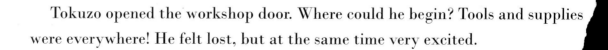

Tokuzo opened the workshop door. Where could he begin? Tools and supplies were everywhere! He felt lost, but at the same time very excited.

德旦打開作坊的門，裡面到處都有工具和材料，但是怎麼開始第一步呢？德旦有些茫然，同時他又很興奮。

Old Master Craftsman was not feeling well, but he was happy to give Tokuzo some advice. "Clay is the best material for your statues, and my workshop has everything you will need. You are welcome to stay there. Unfortunately, you'll have to work by yourself, because I am too sick to help you."

老工匠在病中，但是很高興指教德旦。他說：「泥土是做雕塑的最好材料，我的作坊裡有你需要的一切，歡迎你到我的作坊來，可惜我身體不好，不能親自幫忙，你只有自己動手了。」

A few weeks later, Tokuzo perfected his cat. "Look, everyone! I did it! My dream has finally come true!"

Old Master Craftsman came running from his bed. "Good job! You did it!" he exclaimed.

His daughter was cheering, too. "How wonderful! My father is running without his cane! Tokuzo, your cat has chased his pain away!"

幾個星期後，德旦的雕塑貓變得十分完美。「大家都來看！我做成功了！我的夢想終於成真了！」

老工匠也下床跑出來，大聲稱讚：「真棒，你做得非常好。」老工匠的女兒也非常激動：「真是太好了，我爸爸沒有撐拐棍就跑出來，看來你的貓驅趕走我爸爸的病痛。」

It happened that Old Master's daughter was a talented painter. So she helped decorate the statues. "This cat has a whole new life of its own!" Tokuzo was thrilled. They named the cat *Maneki Neko*, which means "The Cat That Invites Good Luck."

老工匠的女兒碰巧是個有靈氣的畫家，她給雕塑繪了彩色。「這只貓有了它自己全新的生命。」德旦非常激動，他們給這只貓起了新名字「幸運貓，」意思是「帶來好運氣的貓」。

Soon, *Maneki Neko* statues spread all over Japan, and everybody wanted to have one. As time passed, people started to say that a raised right paw brings fortune, and a raised left paw brings happiness and good luck.

　很快，幸運貓雕塑的名聲就傳遍全日本。每個人都想擁有一只幸運貓。隨著時光流逝，一種說法漸漸地傳開：舉起右爪的貓，會招財進寶；舉起左爪的貓，會帶來快樂和好運氣。

"*Osho-san*, did Tama really die?" Old Master asked.

"Well, the body can die, but the *kokoro* lives forever. Therefore, Tama can always remain in our hearts."

This story of the *Maneki Neko* reminds us that what we do is the cause of tomorrow. Even a tiny kitten might remember what we do. And it might even save our life. Or it might just be a friend forever and ever.

老工匠問老和尚:「圓圓真的死了嗎?」

「是啊,身體是死亡了,可是精靈卻能夠永存。所以說,圓圓將永遠活在我們心中。」

幸運貓的故事告訴我們今天的行為和明天發生的事情有因果關係。即使一只小貓也會記住我們的作為。日後,它可能會救我們的命,或者它會成為我們的朋友,那種永久永久的朋友。